Copyright © 2010

make believe ideas ltd

The Wilderness, Berkhamsted, Hertfordshire, HP4 2AZ, UK.
565 Royal Parkway, Nashville, TN 37214, USA.

Illustrated by Kate Toms.
Designed by Annie Simpson.

The Wheels on the Bus

go round and round

Kate Toms

make believe ideas

The wheels on the bus go round and round, round and round, round and round.

LIBRARY

The **wheels** on the bus go round and round, all day long!

go round and round

The **driver** on the bus says,

All aboard,

all aboard,

all aboard.

The **driver** on the bus says,

All aboard,

all day long!

The **babies** on the bus go
wah, wah, wah,
wah, wah, wah,
wah, wah, wah!

The **babies** on the bus go
wah, wah, wah,

all day long!

go round and round

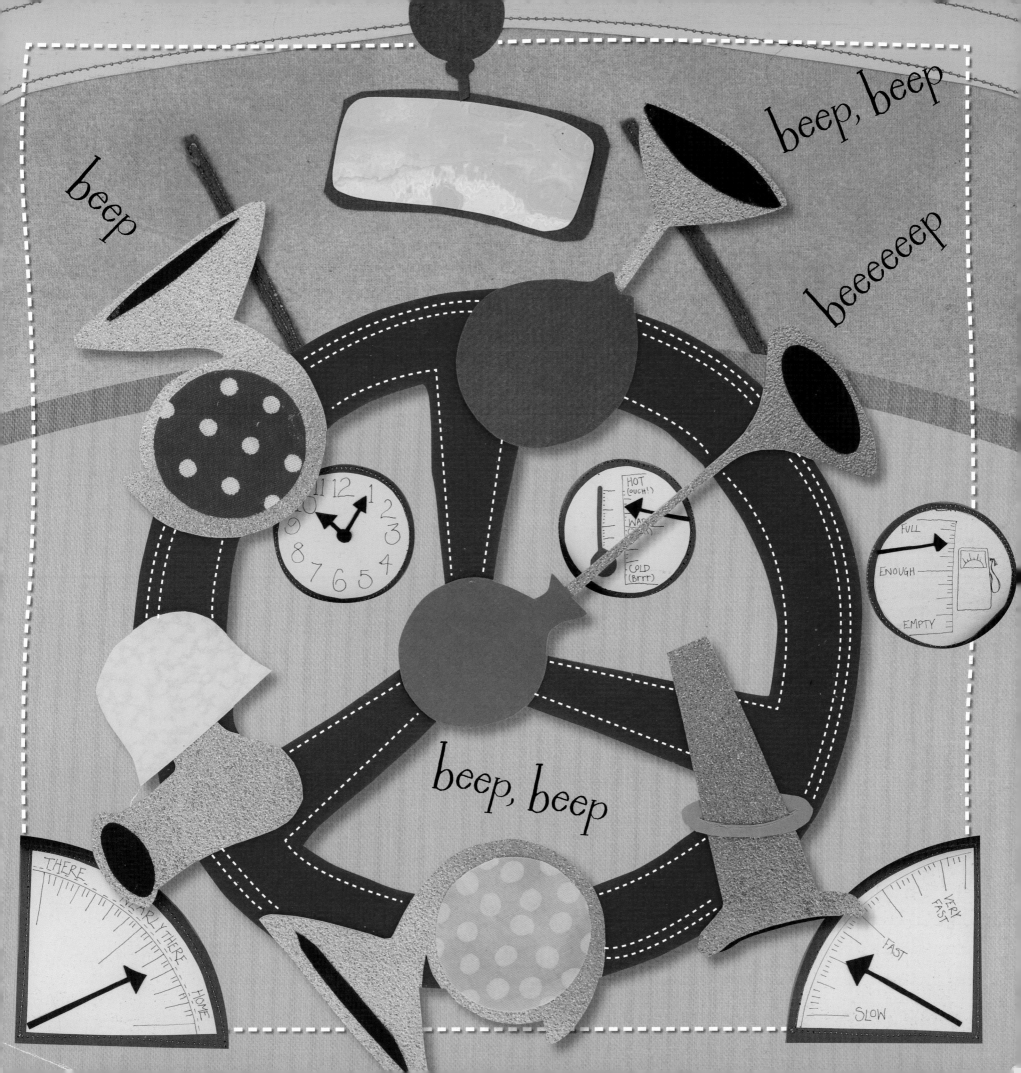

The **mommies** on the bus go

cluck, cluck, cluck,

cluck, cluck, cluck,

cluck, cluck, cluck.

The **mommies** on the bus go

cluck, cluck, cluck,

all day long!

go round and round

The children on the bus jump up and down, up and down, up and down.

The children on the bus jump up and down, all day long!

The **daddies** on the bus say,
Please sit still!
Please sit still!
Please sit still!

The **daddies** on the bus say,
Please sit still!
all day long!

go round and round

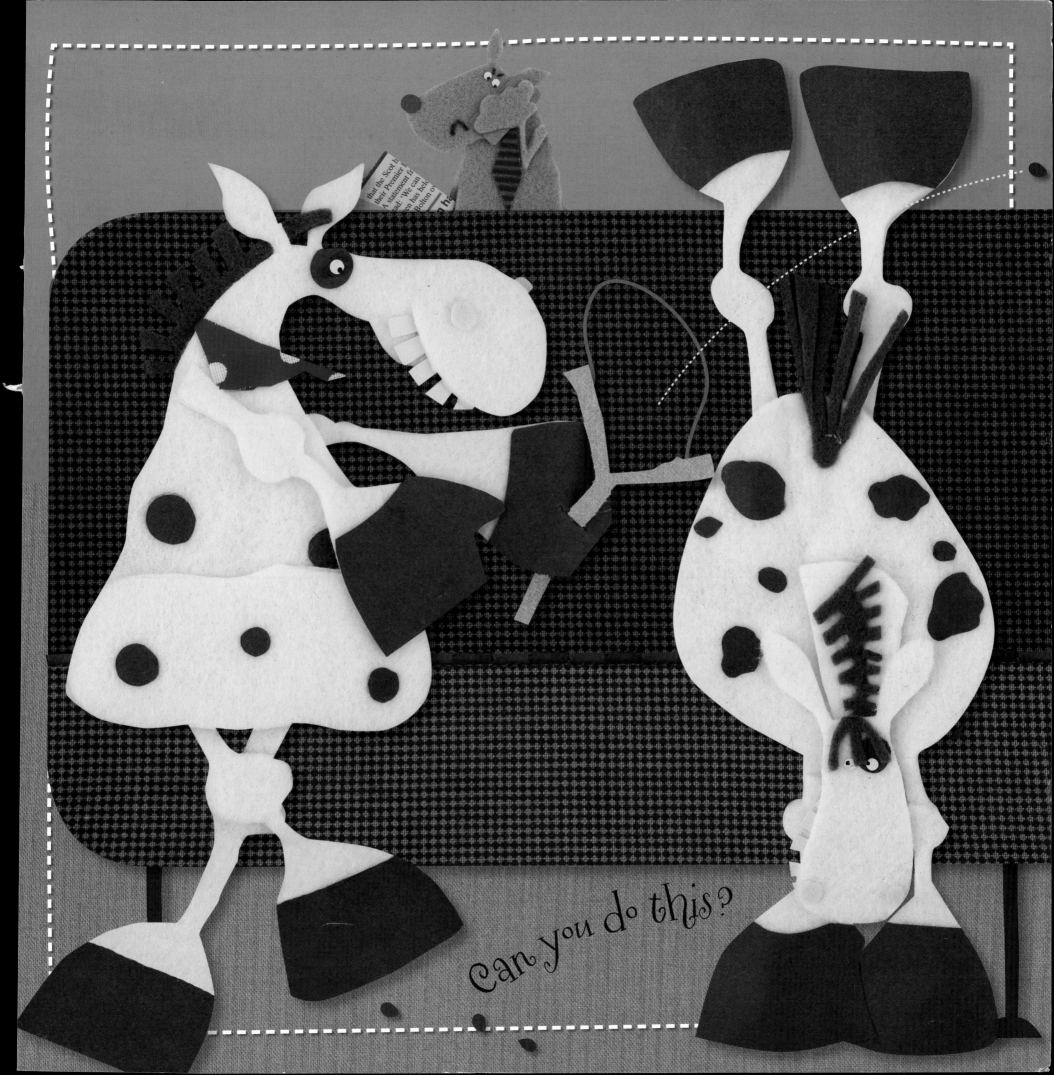

Can you do this?

The **wheels** on the bus go round and round, round and round, round and round. The **wheels** on the bus go round and round, all day long!

bye-bye!